D1017400

PIP AND THE
WOOD WITCH CURSE

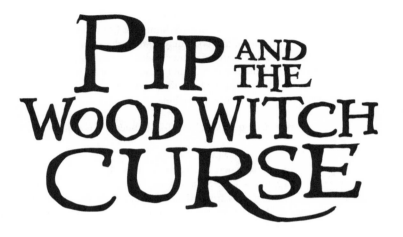

PIP AND THE WOOD WITCH CURSE

CHRIS MOULD

ALBERT WHITMAN & COMPANY
CHICAGO, ILLINOIS

First published in the UK by Hodder Children's Books, a division of Hachette
Children's Books.
Published in 2012 by Albert Whitman & Company.
Printed in China.

Library of Congress Cataloging-in-Publication Data

Mould, Chris.
Pip and the wood witch curse / Chris Mould.
p. cm.— (The Spindlewood tales ; bk. 1)
Summary: After running away from an orphanage, Pip arrives in the walled
city of Hangman's Hollow, where children must hide to avoid imprisonment
bycitizens or danger from evil creatures in the surrounding forest, but new
friend Toad asks his help in finding a lone girl.
ISBN 978-0-8075-6548-3 (alk. paper)
[1. Adventure and adventurers—Fiction. 2. Magic—Fiction. 3.
Orphans—Fiction. 4. Supernatural—Fiction.] I. Title.
PZ7.M85895Piw 2012
[Fic]—dc23
2012013165
10 9 8 7 6 5 4 3 2 1 BP 16 15 14 13 12

For more information about
Albert Whitman & Company,
visit our Web site at www.albertwhitman.com.

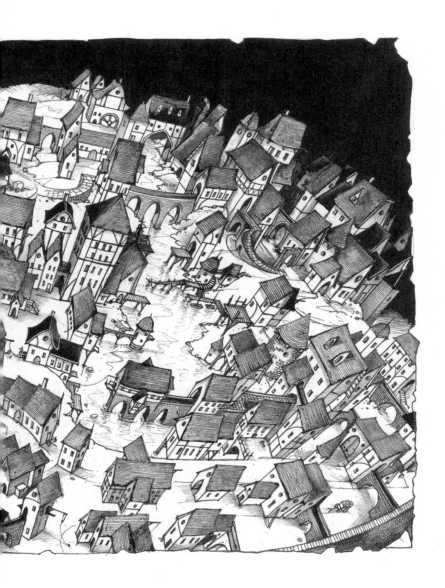

EXPLAINING HOW EDDIE PIPKIN CAME TO HANGMAN'S HOLLOW

Perhaps you have heard of Hangman's Hollow. The great walled city, first built as a place of refuge for the valley people, with its crooked buildings crammed into winding streets and alleyways. Where twisted spires point like broken branches into the air beside the crumbling chimney pots, and smoke pipes up from the hovels, fusing into the clouds. A great river cuts the city in two and a dark

1

forest creeps up around the edges, spilling its dreamy nightmare influence over the people. The winters are long there and cold too.

It is no place for you or me, and it was nothing more than fate that delivered a small helpless boy inside its creaking gates one dreadful winter's night.

Oakes Orphanage, some considerable time ago. Such a desperately long time ago, in fact, that even the crumbling bones of your oldest relatives would have had no recollection of such an era.

Darkness fell. Daylight was replaced by a handful of meager candle stubs burning at the table. A scuffed, leather-bound book was opened and a dirty hand ran down a long list. A forefinger stopped on the name *Eddie Pipkin* and an inky line was scratched through the middle.

"Ah well, that's one mouth we don't have to feed," came a voice, pausing to swig from a grog bottle. "And the money should keep us goin' for a while, Mrs. Tulip. Have you got the little urchin's things ready?"

"Yes, Mister Oakes." A short round woman with a

toothless grin came scurrying, limping slightly on one leg. She plonked a bundle bound with twine onto the tabletop.

"Where is he?"

"Right here." She stepped out into the hallway and pulled someone by his collar into the candlelit room. The teary-eyed youngster was almost thrown off his feet. He straightened himself up and yanked his shirt back into place, trying desperately not to blubber.

Eddie Pipkin was ten years old and small for his age. He had large brown eyes and a pale complexion that was topped with a ruffle of short, dark, wild hair.

"You ready to go to sea, young Pip?"

"No, sir. Not at all!"

"No! What do you mean, no?"

"I don't want to go to sea, Mister Oakes. Not with Captain Snarks. I don't want to be a pirate's cabin boy. Anyway, I'll get seasick and I won't be no good to anyone."

"Master Pipkin, calm yourself. Now let me tell you this for the last time," said Oakes, leaning his face into young Pip's until his foul breath almost made the boy retch. "Firstly, Captain Snarks ain't no pirate. I don't

3

deal wi' crooks or villains."

Pip knew this to be a lie. Oakes would sell his own mother to a highwayman if the money was right.

"Secondly, me and Mrs. Tulip 'ave looked after you since you was a tiny baby. And now we 'as to look after other tiny babies. 'Ow d'you expect us to look after other tiny babies if we ain't got no money? This orphanage won't run itself," he spluttered.

Pip took a good long look at Oakes, who could barely take care of himself, never mind being responsible for the welfare of young children. And Pip was sure that selling children off was no way to raise money.

"I don't know, Mister Oakes, but can't I go to somebody else? I could carry on with my work at the stable yard?"

4

"You can do as you're told, Pipkin, that's what you can do. Stable yard won't pay me good enough money. Now get yer things and I'll take you down to the 'arbor. You set sail in the morning at high tide."

Deep down Pip knew that come hell or high water, he would not be going to sea with Captain Snarks. He just needed to find the right moment to escape, and he knew that Oakes always drank more when he knew that money was coming.

Pip was tied like a dog with a fine rope around his middle. Old Oakes wobbled along drunkenly, hanging on to the other end, mumbling away, and slurring his words as they meandered down to the harbor in the dark.

"You've always been a good lad, Pip. I'll miss you," he said, and each sentence finished with a hiccup. "I remember when you came to us. Such a tiny baby, wrapped in rags, left in the snow. So beautiful." He began to cry pathetically.

Pip took no notice. Always the same—a few drinks and the tales came out and the emotions started. Oakes was doddering around in the dark, wobbling this way and that.

5

Pip slowed up to cut some slack on his leash and stop it from pulling at his middle. He looked ahead and saw the dark shape of Snark's sinister schooner looming down at them. It was huge and just to look at its awesome size sent a shiver running through him.

Voices came from the deck. Barrels and boxes were hoisted on ropes and silhouettes climbed up and down the ladders.

"Please, Mister Oakes. I don't want to go to sea."

That alone was enough to sever the short length of Oakes' temper. "You don't know how lucky you are, Pipkin. Saved from near death and given a life o' luxury. Some folks would give anything to climb aboard a great ship and sail the seven seas. Feel the salt water splashing against their face—" ... And as he spoke the words he lost his footing at the harbor's edge and dropped feet-first into the freezing water.

He was barely visible in the darkness, but the splash and ripple helped Pip pick him out. Pip stood motionless for a moment, trying to take in what had just happened. He could see Oakes' head and shoulders and his large coat spread out on the water's surface.

"'Elp, lad. Get me out. Fetch Captain Snarks!" Oakes screamed. He was gasping and floundering in the depths of the water. "Don't leave old Papa Oakes in the water, Pip!"

But a huge grin broke across Pip's face. He looked down to see the other end of his leash trailing loose. He untied it and watched it drop into the foam. Then without hesitation he turned and walked slowly away, not believing his luck. And as it dawned on him that he was free, he began to move faster. And faster and faster until he was bolting like a sewer rat through the streets of Ludge Port. In the distance, Oakes' cry echoed through the twists and turns of the alleyways, eventually fading into a wonderful silence.

Pip stole away from the coast, heading inland, not sure where he was going but knowing that to stay put was to seal his fate. His arms were still full of his belongings. His short legs powered upward as he climbed the grassy slope that led to the road. His breath made clouds around his face. He dropped half his things as he went but dared not stop, not even for the briefest moment.

Soon he was treading the stony winding road and, capturing his breath, he looked down on the town below. A growing sense of freedom washed over him as he watched the candlelit windows of Oakes Orphanage become small flecks of glimmering yellow.

He pushed on, puffing and panting, fearing that as soon as the authorities found out they would be on to him, tracking him with hounds and horses. Trailing after him through the dark.

He imagined them following. He thought he could hear their voices, feel the thunder of hooves upon the road, and see the glimmer of torchlight held aloft in the blackness. And even though he knew he was only imagining it, it urged him on, until he was far from anywhere he knew.

At length he slowed into a walk. He kept stopping to bundle together his things, tying them tighter and hoicking them higher up on his back, puffing and panting. Only the moonlight showed the way, a pale washed-out yellow spilling along the road ahead, urging him onward. The moon was on his side, he thought.

There was a rumble in the distance. Pip stopped.

Listened. His heart quickened and he heard that too.
He looked back and now he could see horses and the
swinging torchlights he had imagined. His felt his knees
weaken in panic, but in a moment he realized that what
was coming up the road toward him was not a search party
but a slow-moving train of old carriages.

He hung back from the road and lay poised, silent,
and foxlike in the undergrowth. Two black mares struggled
up front against the growing incline. The wheels were
skidding in the dust and the carriages rocked and swayed,
the horses braying and blowing hot breath like smoke.
Silhouettes of people filed out and began pushing from the
back. The wheels bit harder into the road and the train
moved smoothly again.

Lettering became visible on the side of the first
carriage. *Stage Fright Theatre Company—dancing
masters of the macabre.*

Some kind of traveling show, thought Pip. Perhaps he
should take the chance and climb aboard, get away as fast
as possible. But he knew he must remain hidden. Who
knows who these people were? He would use them for the
ride and bail out when it was safe to do so.

Whilst the train still moved slowly he made a move to climb into the rear carriage, taking a chance and not knowing what would greet him. He hooked on to the back, trotting for a moment and looking for something to lunge onto and take a hold. With both hands held tight around the canvas he pulled himself upward and lowered his feet down onto the carriage platform. And then, unthreading the canvas at the corner, he stole inside to find himself scrabbling around in a sea of theater props. It was pitch black but he felt the curious things around him and guessed at what they were. Masks and helmets. Long coats and gowns. Swords and shields.

He heard distant voices from the other carriages, laughing and joking and telling their tales. In the early hours he fell asleep to the gentle swaying of the coach.

The journey was long and tough. Days rolled into nights and back into days again. At times they stopped and lit fires, cooked, and ate and sang songs. They told their tales as Pip listened from beneath the canvas. Dark and dreadful they were, of beasts and ogres and strange lands

where the wild winds blew and thunder bellowed through the mountains. Of storms at sea and the wicked ways of men. Of dragons and kings and circles of magic.

Pip would have given anything to have joined them. He grew hungry and weak and longed for good food and the luxury of a campfire. To keep himself warm he had wrapped some kind of animal skin around himself. While the travelers slept he would sneak out and stretch his limbs, grabbing the bones from around the fire and sucking out their flavor.

When he looked around him he knew nothing of the barren lands through which they passed. He would not be leaving their company just yet, not until he found some-where that he felt was safe.

Pip thought of many things along the way. He imagined the perfect life with a real family: brothers and sisters, friends to spend time with, loving parents. Things he had never known. A sense of belonging.

When he slept the same dream returned to him, the one he had always had. There he was, sitting by the hearth, taking in the warmth of a slowly burning fire. His parents were at his side, but try as he might he could not make out their faces. The harder he looked, the more the image became blurred. When he spoke to them he received no answer. And then he watched in frustration as they faded slowly, until they were not there at all.

He would wake in a cold sweat, breathing heavily and hoping he hadn't called out in his sleep.

Pip's only proof that someone actually drove the carriage he was in was the sound of voices bellowing at the black mares.

Though he could not see, there were times when he was sure they were creeping along dangerous precipices or braving the delicate surfaces of frozen lakes. The wind blew harder and the temperature dropped to freezing depths.

It must have been somewhere in the early hours of the morning when the Stage Fright Theatre Company made it home.

A small spy hatch opened and a keen eye peered out.

"Who is it? Whaddya want? ... Oh, it's you lot. Hold on."

A great creak of opening gates echoed around Pip.

He felt the jolt of movement as the carriages pulled forward. There was no mistaking it, they were now inside the walls of a city.

Pip could not have known, but it was a place he had once heard of in a fairy tale. A place they called Hangman's Hollow.

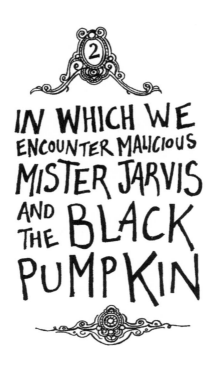

IN WHICH WE ENCOUNTER MALICIOUS MISTER JARVIS AND THE BLACK PUMPKIN

Sooner or later, everyone catches a glimpse of Mister Jarvis. If you only half-looked you might think that he carried a blade by his side, but look again and you'd see that what shone when the light chanced upon it was the hook where his left hand should be. Closer still and you'd see the pink scar it had left across his face when he'd been thrown from his horse. Still, he was proud of that hook.

15

Cleaned it, polished it, buffed it up like a favorite pair of old boots, ready to use should the need arise.

And the rest of him? Always the same wolfskin cloak and long black hair, ragged boots with worn-out soles. Cold and cutthroat he was, and filled with more hatred than the worst of storybook pirates.

Mostly he came at night, but sometimes to catch you unawares he would rattle through the streets in the daylight. Rolling along in the black carriage with his snake eyes peeled on every nook and cranny. Thundering over the cobblestones, sometimes squeezing through the skinny waists of the dark alleyways on foot with only the glow of his lamp to give him away and his cloak flapping out behind him. Or climbing up onto ledges and peering through windows.

And when the rain lashed the streets and the wind hurled itself recklessly around the tiles and chimneys, still he came.

It was winter now and it had snowed all day, thick and fast until it felt like the whole world had been transformed. A sleepy scene of cold, calm peace. As it grew dark, torchlights glowed at doorways and through the

windows, fires burned within. Soft white flakes drifted dreamily downward. All was blissfully quiet.

And then the moment was spoiled. Jarvis's carriage squeaked lazily down Pig Pudding Lane, plowing through the white, spoiling the clean surface with wheel tracks and hoof marks. The coach was squat and round so that it almost resembled a black pumpkin on wheels.

Sliding into the corner, it hung a right turn and entered the emptiness of the square, pulling up slowly. A crow swooped down from the blackness above and settled on Jarvis's hood.

"Well?"

"Well, what?" grumbled Jarvis, disgruntled at the day's pickings.

18

"Did you see anything?"

"No, Esther, I did not. Nothing at all, yet again. Anyway, never mind me. What about you? You're supposed to be my eyes and ears, you useless old buzzard!"

"*Crow*," corrected Esther.

But he was lost in thought and didn't hear. "There are no children here anymore!" he mumbled under his foggy breath.

It was such a long time since he'd caught one that he almost believed it was true, but deep down he knew they were here somewhere. He would find one before the month was out. He'd made that promise to himself already.

He was certainly due some good luck, and he felt his reputation in the hollow was beginning to slide.

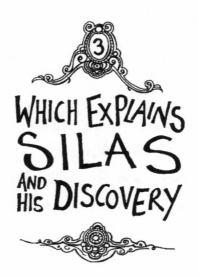

WHICH EXPLAINS SILAS AND HIS DISCOVERY

Pip had no idea what to expect, except that he knew the snow was thicker here. He heard the crunch beneath the wheels and felt the slipping and sliding of the carriages.

Much winding and twisting followed. Perhaps they were close to stopping, most likely working their way down some back alley.

They halted abruptly.

A crunch and squeak of feet came through the snow and a soft glow was visible. Pip could hear a blur of conversation through the whistling wind.

A sniffing sound came close. Pip ducked his head and tried to quell the noise of his rumbling stomach. Something brushed against the canvas and then a slimy voice cut through the thin air.

"I can smell them. They've been here. I'd know that rotten stink anywhere. Mr. Van Delf, you have something on board!"

"Theater props, Mister Jarvis. Nothing but theater props. We go through this every time. Now if you don't mind, it is the dead of night!"

"I'll take a look, if you don't mind." Pip heard the canvas being untied at the corner and saw the light grow stronger as a lamp was lifted inside. He held his eyes shut tight and stayed as still as possible. A moan of disappointment was all that Pip heard before the canvas flap dropped back into place.

Jarvis turned away leery-eyed, snarling and mumbling to himself. He knew that something wasn't right. That nose of his was too trustworthy to be wrong.

He walked away, his cloak trailing in the snow.

The train of carriages continued before coming to a stop nearby in a courtyard of tall timber-framed houses. Pip listened carefully as the horses were stabled and people moved around in the dark. What if they unveiled him right there and then? Whatever would he do?

But the noise died down and the voices petered out. The crunch of feet stepping into the distance was the last thing he heard.

Pip waited. For a good while longer he stayed where he was, but eventually the stiffness in his body was unbearable. His first few movements were painful as he lifted the flap and an icy wind rushed through him. He felt around in the dark, reached for the animal skin, and clambered out, knocking things here and there. Snowflakes were falling softly.

If you had been there as Pip emerged you would not have seen a small boy. You would have seen a dreadful creature with hog's teeth and a wolf's head, stepping awkwardly through the thick snow and laying the most frightening shadows across the doorways of the buildings as, for the first time, Pip discovered the wonders of Hangman's Hollow.

*

Jarvis was long gone by now. If he had waited longer, he too would have seen the beast, creeping along in the snow with the drifts sweeping up around him. But he had grown tired and now he was slumped into his chair with his feet on the brickwork of the fireplace. Meager flames struggled and he held the flat of his right hand out to salvage what heat he could from the embers, his fingerless glove outstretched.

"I'm getting close, Esther. I'll find them. Wherever they are, *who*ever they are. I'll find them all."

"Such a long time since you had any success," Esther croaked. "Not a single prisoner in the forest keep, not for a long time. And to think the last ones escaped … Dear oh dear! Perhaps you've lost your touch." Her feet were clamped to the mantelpiece and she preened her feathers with her beak. She did love to wind his cogs, but it always came at a cost.

"Feathered freak!" he spluttered.

He pulled the hook from his arm and hurled it toward her. It missed and lodged itself into an oak timber as she scampered across the lintel, sending papers and candlesticks crashing into the hearth.

"*And* you've lost your patience," she continued.

He ignored her and went back to warming his one hand.

Silas was different. There was a stillness about him, a
brooding presence that somehow set him apart from
the others.

"All crows are equal," Esther would squawk, but Silas
knew how inadequate she felt in his company.

He was always the first to know about everything. It
was his keen eye, and his patience. So of course it was he
who found something in the snow, something that made
his heart thud and that he knew would set the woods alight
with excitement.

Pip could see only a snowy-white labyrinth of streets and
alleyways, fairy-tale towers and winding stone staircases.
Lantern lights spread a magical orange glow across
everything. Here and there, where the overhangs jutted
out, the snow was only a fine layer and for a moment it felt
good to walk on solid ground.

But there was a feeling as he walked, a sensation of dark and emptiness. As if something had happened here, something that killed the fairy-tale magic of the winding streets.

The draw of torchlight lured him through an archway and up some steps, with his hog's teeth pointing forward and the brush of his tail dusting behind him.

A tall, wide building loomed down at Pip, with little windows and a low squat door with huge hinges that swirled and curved. A faded sign creaked gently overhead—the Deadman's Hand.

What happened next sent Pip's heart racing at such a rate that it felt like it might, at any minute, pop out of his top pocket.

A hand lunged at him from a half-open door and pulled him quickly inside.

It had taken him by the scruff of the neck and lifted him right off his feet, hauling him in like a rag doll. The door slammed shut. A mound of snow fell from somewhere above and landed with a soft thump upon the ground.

Pip looked up. He was now arranged untidily among a collection of small wooden barrels with his arms and legs in knots. Attached to the other end of the arm was a huge man, tall and wide with a wedge of black hair and spectacles perched on his nose.

"You should be more careful, son!" he said, pulling Pip back onto his feet.

"But wha—"

"Don't talk. Move," he continued as he pushed Pip off through the back rooms of the inn.

Back outside, Silas had heard the crunch of footsteps

through the snow. He had been sleeping soundly in the recess of an archway but he was always on alert, even when he rested.

He took a moment to come around before he flew silently through the air, stretching out the long fingers of his wings and following the disturbance upon the ground. Up he went, through Cleaver's Walk and into Stones Alley.

He rested atop an ugly, carved stone face that served the spouts and gutters of the priory roof. He looked down, tucking his beak into the plumes of his chest. Under the dance of lamplight Silas hopped downward with his wings out until he was up close and inspected the imprints that broke the perfect layer of white. His head lifted to one side.

There in the snow were the smallest footprints he had seen in a long time. Perfectly formed, deep and crisp and clear.

"Children ... on the move!" he cawed excitedly, in a long low sneer. "Children indeed. And by the looks of it, only moments ago!"

As the snow continued and covered up the fact that

the prints had ever been there at all, he raised his wings once more and set off excitedly toward the Spindlewood, where he knew he could barter with his newfound wisdom.

CONCERNING DETAILS OF A SHORT CONVERSATION AT THE DEADMAN'S HAND

Pip saw everything fleetingly. A large room with a roaring fire and shadows of drinkers stooped over tables or nestling in the alcoves. Noise spilling out from every corner. The stale smell of ale and tobacco hanging in the air. Thuds and clunks and clangs mixed with shouts and bellowing laughter and the gentle hum of background music from a fiddler.

"My name is Sam," said the huge man. "Where are you from?"

"Not here," said Pip. "Far away!"

"How on earth did you get inside these walls, boy? Didn't your mother ever warn you about Hangman's Hollow?"

"I don't have a mother, sir."

"What's your name then?"

"My name is Eddie Pipkin, but everyone calls me Pip. Did you say Hangman's Hollow? The place where—" But he was cut off.

"Look, Pip, just don't make any noise. Stay here," Sam urged, squeezing him into a small cupboard. "When it grows quiet I'll bring you something to eat."

"Thank you ... I think!"

"You'd have frozen to death out there," said Sam. He was about to leave when he turned back.

"Listen. If you understand nothing else, make sure you understand this. There are no children here. You mustn't let *them* find you."

He closed the door and Pip was left alone in the darkness. And as he sat and waited he wondered about all the things he had heard about the hollow.

A Quiet Word in Your Ear Before Chapter Five

In the still silence of an old cloth sack sat the old wooden soldier. He waited patiently among the odds and ends, with only darkness to keep him company. The years had scratched flakes of paint from his uniform and scuffed the tips of his boots, the once-proud plume in his hat was crooked and lifeless. And he was sleeping soundly until something woke him. *Click-click*. The lids opened. Two eyes shifted from side to side. "There are children on the move," he thought to himself. "Somewhere in the depths of the hollow. Escaping!" But having just awoken, he was not sure where from, or where to. And anyway, there was no one there to tell. He closed his eyes, *click-click*, and fell quickly back to sleep.

AT WHICH POINT WE DISCOVER THINGS LURKING IN THE FOREST

There was something unearthly about the forest at night.
Strange knockings, wood against wood. Distant cackling.
The breaking of branches and all manner of noises that
hinted at sinister goings-on under cover of darkness.
Heavy snow covered the carpet of leaves that autumn had
scattered. Vague shapes shifted through the trees. The eyes
of wolves shone through the black. Shrills and squawks

pierced the air and if you listened carefully, words seemed to whisper along the branches.

Silas was perched on a low bough. He knew it would not be long before he was seen. Something was clinging to a nearby tree, its tattered black cloak draped across the frosted bark. It had its head cocked to one side and one keen green eye staring through the strands of its long hair. Clawed hands loosened their grip on the gnarled wood and the creature scuttled across to meet him.

"Silas! What brings you back to the wood?" she asked. Her voice was sharp and throaty.

"I'm growing hungry,

Hogwick," he announced. "It is some time since I have eaten."

"Dear Silas," she said, drawing a hand out from under her cloak and stroking his plumage, "I think perhaps you have brought news with you."

"Maybe."

"No, not maybe." She grinned and he could see her excitement at the thought that there was something to tell. It was only a moment before more wood witches came, emerging from the hollows of the trees, scrabbling on all fours across the forest floor to meet with their sister, and then standing on two feet to lift themselves up to where Silas was perched. The first, Esmie, was blind and older than the rest. She was skinny and frail, a real bag of old bones. The second, named Pugg, was the opposite, large and round.

Esmie tilted her head to one side and waited. "Come on, come on. Out with it, Silas." She cackled excitedly, showing her crooked teeth.

"Quiet," said Hogwick. "Silas belongs to me. I cannot remember the last time your companions brought us anything useful. Now let the bird have his say."

"I have seen and heard something this very night," Silas announced, "but my belly aches so much with hunger I do not think I can get the words out."

"Stay there, Silas. Don't move." Hogwick skipped away, retrieving something from inside the hollow of a tree. They watched him swallow it whole.

"Perhaps a little more," he persuaded. "The cold nights seem to make me more hungry." And the whole scenario was played out several times before eventually Silas was satisfied and let out his secret.

"Are you sure?" questioned Hogwick excitedly. "A child, you say. A small child!" All three rubbed their hands with glee.

"Children! Oooh, you're making me feel hungry," groaned Pugg. She laughed and set Esmie off doing the same.

"QUIET. Where did the child go?" asked Hogwick, trying her best to dampen the excitement.

"Mmmmm … I'm not sure. The snowfall has been heavy but beneath the overhangs its thickness peters out and the trail is lost," Silas said. "It is hard to tell but the tracks were fresh and ran past the priory."

"Keep an eye out," Hogwick said, "and I shall do the same, and be sure to come and seek me out if you grow hungry again."

The witches disappeared into the velvet black of the forest, trailing their feet through the white carpet and chattering to themselves.

THE BIT AT THE END OF CHAPTER FIVE

"There is nothing worse than a fitful sleep." The old wooden soldier tossed and turned in the cloth sack. He'd had the same dream for several nights. At first, a girl all alone in the darkness. And now a small boy, lost and far from home, his tiny footprints embedded in the snow. If he thought hard enough he knew he could find them all, every last one of them, and one day soon he probably would. *Click-click.* He drifted back into sleep.

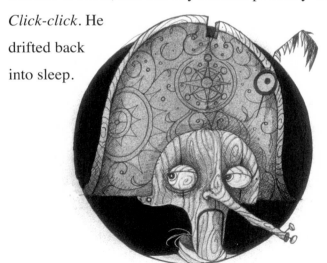

IN WHICH AN EXPLANATION IS OFFERED BY THE INNKEEPER

It must have been the early hours of the morning when Pip heard the latch lift on the cupboard door. He'd been worn out and weather-beaten into a fitful sleep, but for how long he wasn't sure.

Sam took him to the large open room of the tavern, stocked with barrels and tankards, with candles flickering at the tables. Portraits of city folk were dotted around the room on the cracked plaster and it seemed as if the place had been furnished with whatever could be found. Church pews, wing-backed chairs, seats and tables made from barrels. But it was snug and warm and felt like a homely place.

The inn had emptied and the only sound came from the dying fire as it spat and crumbled.

Sam stared at the fire and Pip watched his face grow hypnotized by the flames.

"They say they used to hang people here, in those woods," Sam began. "Bad people. From those twisted boughs that creak and groan in the wind. And they say that all the badness from those people somehow found its way into those old Spindlewood trees, so deep that it planted its evil right down into the spiny roots. And that's where those things came from."

"What things?" asked Pip, who was now perched on the edge of his chair.

"You don't know *anything* about this place, do you Pip?"

"No sir, not at all. Once I heard of this place in a fairy tale. But the tale was so dark and twisted that I presumed the place didn't exist and that none of it was true!"

"Let me start at the beginning, Pip. Long ago."

They sat huddled up to the hearth and Sam gave Pip a plate of something hot. He ate it so fast he barely took any notice of what it was, and sat back in his huge chair.

"It's a hundred years now since these streets were newly laid," said Sam, who was easing gently into his tale. "Craftsmen came to build up the timber frames and lay the stone. Cobbled walkways were sunk into the dry earth. Rooflines poked into the sky and chimney pots belched out smoke as the streets filled with people. The city was new then and there was

the happiness that comes with a fresh start. For a good while it was peaceful, but then something awoke in the forest. The trees began to creak and groan. Not the creak and groan that is normal for a tree when the wind blows or the branches stretch out to grab hold of the sunlight. No, a painful long-lasting sound that signified some sort of change.

"Hollows appeared in many of the trees. People claimed that something had hatched out from the Spindlewood. A darkness hung about the forest and the air turned heavy and oppressive. Animals disappeared from the woods and the birdsong stopped. Rumors whispered among the people and soon even the hardest of hunters and woodsmen were afraid to enter.

"And then they came. Creatures from the forest, wood witches, and other things, creatures of all kinds and in great numbers."

Pip shivered and moved a little closer to the fire.

Surely what Sam told him wasn't true, it was just a story to teach him a lesson.

Wasn't it?

"I don't do fairy stories," said Sam. "Not at this time

of night!"

He watched the boy's expression and let the tale sink in.

"Did you say *creatures*?" asked Pip.

"You heard me right," said Sam. "Creatures. All kinds of things that lurk and skulk in the twilight, that nest in shadowed streets and prey upon those foolish enough to venture out."

Suddenly, Pip's home in the Oakes Orphanage and even the cabin aboard Snark's pirate ship seemed like heaven. He had gone from bad to worse.

"I should go from here," he started. "Right now."

"That's not as easy as you might think, young Pip. Even if you made it through the city to the gates, they would turn you over to the authorities. Any children discovered in the hollow are imprisoned until they are old enough to fight against the forest armies. And any adults found concealing children face a far worse fate!"

"What! But can't you smuggle me out?" asked Pip, with a lump well and truly placed in his throat.

"And then what? You're so far from anywhere you would perish if you tried to make it alone, and if I was caught they'd hang me at the gallows."

"I thought that tales of beasts and witches belonged in storybooks," exclaimed Pip, staring deeply into the fire.

"Of course," said Sam. "But right here is where those stories came from!

"Where the forest meets the city there is a gate. In the past, people left things there, for the beasts, of course. They believed it would prevent them from stealing their children, from making prisoners of them in their bid to take the city.

"I do not wish to frighten you, Pip. But it is important that you stay safe. Children are becoming a thing of the past.

When the wars began the creatures emerged from their lairs and took the little ones, imprisoning them in the forest. As the problem grew the people of the city became careful to lock up their young and keep them out of sight. The creatures used their companions to seek out more little ones. Wolves and crows, rooks and ravens. Before long many children were gone and to prevent further disaster no one was allowed to bring children into the hollow.

"Now the streets are empty of young life. Many people still have children and hide them away, but no one knows where or how many or if indeed it is true at all. No man trusts his neighbor. What fool would reveal the hiding place of his most prized possession?

"The authorities search for children too. Young life is a threat to the safety of the city. They come in the night: voices in the early hours, shouts and yells, banging at the doors, shaking the timber frames. Raids, spot checks, call them what you will. It takes a crafty child to escape imprisonment by the authorities.

"For now you must keep your head down. Don't even look through the windows. It's most important you're not seen by the crows. For the taste of an old carcass they would betray your darkest secret."

"What kind of a place is this?" shuddered Pip. "And why are you helping me?"

"It is a place to be feared and avoided," said Sam. "And I am sorry that you came here not knowing that, but now that you are here and in my care, we must make sure you stay hidden. I have my own reasons for helping you.

"If you hear horses' hooves and voices and doors banging in the night, you must be ready to move. Make sure you sleep with your boots on. It's my golden rule."

7

WHEN IT IS REVEALED THAT, SURPRISINGLY, PIP IS NOT ALONE

Pip was left to sleep by the fireside. The shutters were
closed and the burning logs would keep him snug through
the early hours. But the scene was almost like the one from
his dream.

While he slept his parents took their places in the
empty chairs. Twisting knotted branches of Spindlewood
wound around the carved wooden legs. Deadly forest

creatures curled around the tendrils and crawled across the floor.

When he awoke he was sweating. What was this place? He was so haunted by Sam's story that he now wished desperately not to be there at all. He toyed with the idea of leaving in the night, but the thought of meeting something ghastly in the winding streets was too frightening to bear. Flickering firelight caused dark dancing shadows to play on the walls. He closed his eyes tight and curled up in his blanket.

At first light Sam appeared. He'd made a breakfast of eggs and ham with home-baked bread and fresh milk. Funny how things always seemed a little better in the daytime.

"Not so fast, Pip," warned Sam. "You'll make yourself ill. You're safe now. You'll be fed and watered for as long as you're here. Take your time."

"I still don't know why you are being so kind to me," insisted Pip. To be treated so well was something he had never experienced before. Usually, such an act would be accompanied by drunkenness or followed by a beating.

Sam smiled. There was something of the gentle giant

51

about him. He had a huge but calm presence.

When Sam was convinced that Pip had satisfied his appetite, he stood up and beckoned him to follow.

Pip jumped from his chair, wiping his mouth on his sleeve. He followed Sam through the house. They wound up a staircase at the back of the building to the first floor and up a second narrower set to another. The passages grew slimmer and the spaces smaller.

Eventually they reached a turn in the corridor, where what appeared to be a panel turned out to be the entrance to a room at the top of the building. Sam put his hand through what looked like an accidental hole in the wood. He lifted a latch and entered. What Pip saw wasn't what he had expected. There, perched on a makeshift bed, was a boy perhaps slightly older than himself and much bigger, with a portly face and a round belly.

Almost a miniature version of Sam. He jumped up and held out his hand.

"I'm Toad," he said. "Pleased to meet you!" He had a wild look in his eyes and an expression that told Pip it was the first time he had seen another child in some time. He looked somehow familiar and, on closer inspection, Pip realized that he had seen a penciled portrait of him on the wall in the downstairs rooms of the tavern.

Pip stared around the room, taken aback. There were drawings and sheets of writing pinned to the wall, and small models made from wood. Then he looked back at Toad.

"I like to keep busy!" Toad laughed.

"I'm Pip," he replied and they shook hands. The boy Toad seemed genuinely excited at the prospect of his new companion.

"His real name is Thomas," said Sam. "And he's my son. Now you can see why I helped you, Pip. I must attend to the tavern. Keep your heads down and I'll return later." He closed the door and was gone.

"Make yourself at home," said Toad. "You'll be getting to know this place pretty well."

Pip stared around the room. It was tiny. He didn't want to know the place well. He wanted to leave. Toad's bed was a large wooden box filled with sheets and comfortable-looking cushions and pillows. Something similar had been swiftly put together in the opposite corner.

"That's yours," said Toad. "We keep a spare in case we take in any strays from the city."

"Strays?"

"Escaped children, wandering alone. If you don't take them in, they'll be preyed upon by the forest folk or picked up by guardsmen. Either way, you're imprisoned." Toad seemed so matter of fact about the whole thing that Pip felt his stomach turning again and his heart sank into his belly.

"It's an unwritten rule among the elders," claimed Toad. "Or at least, among those who are hiding children. They must all be ready to help each other out should the need occur. It's quite normal."

Pip told Toad his long tale. Of Mister Oakes and the orphanage, and how he had worked at the stables and taken care of the horses, riding through the ravines, splashing through the running water, and heading out over the hills.

"It sounds incredible," said Toad. "One day you'll return and I'll come with you. You can show me how to ride a horse."

Pip stared at Toad. "You're right. It is incredible, but somehow I never realized it, not until now. I would give anything to be back there. I need to get out of here."

There was a tapping at the window in the sloped roof above. Fluttering, cooing.

"Just a dove," said Toad. "I never used to see them, but lately this one has joined me every morning. Sometimes alone, sometimes with others."

They looked up and watched it dance on the tiles, backward and forward at the window. There was a telescope and a curtain with a circular hole in it so that Toad could poke the lens through and look out over the city unnoticed.

"Come and take a look," said Toad. There was a stepladder underneath the window, resting against shelves of books and paper and wooden boxes filled with junk. Toad climbed the stepladder, and Pip joined him on its top step. He stared through the telescope, taking a moment to get used to the view through the lens. He could see the treetops of the forest and the sun melting the rooftop snow. Then he steered downward into the square.

He handed the scope to Toad and watched him push his chubby face into the viewer.

"Why do they call you Toad?" asked Pip.

"Father says if the wood witches ever caught me, that's what they'd turn me into," Toad explained. He looked round at Pip and laughed.

Pip couldn't find it in him to find it amusing just yet. He was still growing used to the idea that the forest creatures existed at all and that he would have to hide for as long as he was here. It felt like a pointless existence.

"Did Father tell you about the Dupries?" asked Toad, who was now wearing a serious expression.

"No."

"Jean Duprie is a friend of my father, a baker in the city. He used to supply us with bread. His house was turned over by the authorities in the night and two of their children were discovered. The house was boarded up and now the children and their parents are held captive."

"What will happen to them?" asked Pip.

"Prison," said Toad. "Concealing children is the worst of crimes here. Children encourage wood creatures into the city. It makes the place unsafe, so they are held in the city prisons until they are older. But they have no right to do that to a family. They are as bad as the beasts in the woods. But there's more to tell you," he continued.

Pip waited, not wanting to bump him off his stride. "Go on," he urged.

"My father knows Jean Duprie very well, well enough to know that he had three children, not two. We fear that his youngest daughter is somewhere in the city, hiding alone. She will not survive for long on her own. We must find her, Pip, without Father knowing that we are leaving the tavern. I need your help."

Concerning an Insight into the Stone Circle

It grew cold again and flurries of snow drifted down at intervals. But excitement boiled in the freezing depths of the woods. Word was passing quickly, from beak to lip, from lip to snout. There had been no sign of a child for such a long time that the sighting had stirred the forest dwellers into a frenzy. So much so that the Stone Circle was called.

In the very heart of the forest sat the ancient remains of a building. Here and there crumbling archways still stood. Moss and lichen lay thick beneath the snow, and thorns and long tendrils pulled at the stonework, almost as if dragging it back into the earth below.

And right here, in the center of the ruin, was the home of the Stone Circle. As the old saying went:

Whosoever comes to the circle must bring rock or stone and place it in the ground. A full circle of stones represents the strength of union in the forest.

Cloudy wisps of frosted fog swirled and drifted around the
clearing. The first arrival held a rock in both hands. She
kissed it for good luck and placed it in the soft snow.
Another followed and for a moment they stood alone in the
darkness watching the moonlight. Then the others came.
The small yellow eyes of the wolves pricked through the
black curtain of night. The crows followed,
descending from above, dusting the snow from the higher
branches as they came. Then witches, scratching their way
down the trunks from their high perches and emerging
from the hollows on all fours like scrabbling insects.

Something padded through the snow. Rolling and rumbling followed, and torchlight sang through the mist. First a black mare, then the pumpkin carriage, then down from his perch stepped the man with the hooked hand and the wolfskin cloak. He entered the circle and took a small pebble from his pocket with his good hand. He polished it against his filthy cloak and placed it down neatly.

A bark demon was clamped on to the back of the pumpkin with its cloak trailing over the wheels. It climbed down, grabbing the torch as it came, crawling awkwardly, bent double. On two legs and one hand it passed across the clearing with the flame held over its head.

A wood witch followed. She wore a skull cap and was wrapped in so much rag and old cloth that only her sunken eyes could be seen. She dragged a small two-wheeled cart whose tracks gave away her winding path from the densest part of the forest.

She pulled a pile of kindling wood from the cart and placed it neatly in the middle of the circle, using the torch to light the fire. For a while there was no sound except the crack and spit of blistering twigs and branches.

Roach came last to the circle. He was long and loose-limbed like Jarvis, but their similarities ended there. He had a second pair of arms positioned under the first so that he appeared not unlike an upright insect. The hands of the second pair swung below his knees and almost reached the forest floor. His long forehead and sharp chin made him frightening for sure, but he was somehow awkward. He used a stick to walk, yet he was swift and skillful in his movement, lightning fast.

He was accompanied by Fenris, leader of the wolf pack. Fenris ambled up to his side and Roach stroked the nape of his neck gently. The wolf's eyes glowed like fireflies, catching the reflection from the yellow moon.

Roach took his stone out from his top pocket, passing it from an upper arm to a lower arm so that he could place it without bending his knees.

Hogwick leaned forward, resting on her stick with both hands.

"Creatures of the forest, I bring news. In these last few days my companion Silas has discovered signs of children. Fresh signs. Trails in the snow. We came close to catching a youngster," she claimed, dressing up her tale, "but harsh weather impeded the hunt. Once again Silas brings hope to the Spindlewood. It is too long since we captured one, but the young still move through the city. Persistence will bring triumph. Use your companions well, they are your eyes and ears."

All of them looked at Silas. Many of the birds stirred with jealousy, and the wolves were determined to succeed in the search for young life.

"There is at least one child that we know of. The Duprie house has been turned over, but one young girl escaped into the city when the authorities failed to find her. Silas brought this news also," she announced proudly.

Jarvis raised one eyebrow at Esther, perched on his shoulder. She ruffled her feathers and ignored his glare.

"The hunt is on. Go now," called Hogwick, "and return with good news. We are all waiting."

9

DURING WHICH A SHORT DISCUSSION IS OVERHEARD

A hooded figure appeared at the tavern doorway, shaking his cloak and kicking snow from his boots. He ordered ale with his head held low and was careful to conceal one hand. He asked for food and sat quietly in a fireside corner where a candle had been melted into the grain of the tabletop. A ripple of hush and whisper ran around the tavern and sly looks fell his way.

Pip and Toad watched in secrecy from the cellar stairs. Toad whispered to Pip, "He's here, the one I told you about. That's him. Let's go." They shrank back into the shadow and crept down the stone steps.

Sam knew it was old Jarvis but there was little he could say or do. He knew he'd be listening for information, hoping the locals might forget themselves and spill a secret here and there when the drinks had gotten the better of them.

In some ways Sam saw it as an opportunity. He was keen to show that everything was as it should be at the tavern. It was plain to see there were no children here!

Jarvis kept an eye on Sam and in return, Sam did the same. In truth, no one trusted Jarvis. He was a traitor. The authorities employed him to seek out children for imprisonment but, disgruntled at his meager wages and fueled by his hatred of the young, he was determined to pass them on to the forest folk. And how did the forest folk pay him? They went in search of what they knew he desired more than anything—money. They raided houses at night, ransacked shops in the dark hours, ambushed market traders if they made their way home late at night. And so things grew worse, all because of Mister Jarvis: the man who had secretly spent so much time double-dealing with the creatures of the forest that he had almost become one himself.

Right now he was keeping warm at the fire. He nursed a tankard of ale and in the flickering shadows he used his hook to spear the food on his plate. Esther stepped out from under his cloak and they whispered under the cracking and spitting of the burning logs.

Unbeknownst to Jarvis and his crow, Pip and Toad were positioned beneath them in the cellar. A hole in the floorboards revealed the underside of Jarvis's leather boot. They listened carefully.

"I want to know where the Duprie child has gone," said Jarvis. "What news do you have?" He brushed some breadcrumbs under her beak.

"I have news from Silas, sir. She is on the move. She may be disguised, but we have no idea how."

"Do you think I am stupid, Esther? Of course she is on the move. Their home has been ransacked. Of course she'll be disguised. Tell me something I don't know and *don't* tell me you paid Silas for that information."

"She may be using the river to pass up and down the

city. There are
rumors of a
small boat."

"What rumors?"

"A boat was tethered
to the Firefly Bridge. It
disappeared at the same
time the Duprie girl went
on the run."

Jarvis stared hard back
at her. "You know I don't
like water."

"Maybe she doesn't
like it either. She may
have been forced to row
upstream to avoid the city
folk."

"Esther, if
you feel sym-
pathy toward
those little
rats, don't ever

let it slip in front of me. If I ever lay my hands on that dreadful child she will wish she had perished in that water."

Toad looked at Pip and Pip stared back. Jarvis really was the villain that Toad had described. He really did hate children.

"If she escapes outside the city gates she'll never make it alive. I'll bet my shiny hook that she is heading into the heart of the hollow," said Jarvis. "The day I rid this place of all its children will be a happy one. Ah, if only we could find Captain Dooley," he sighed, sipping at the froth of his ale. "Then all our troubles would be solved."

"No one knows where Captain Dooley is. Not even Silas," Esther assured him.

"Captain Dooley?" whispered Pip, staring questioningly at Toad. "Who on earth is Captain Dooley?"

Toad held his finger to his lips. "Later," he whispered.

Just then Esther spilled Jarvis's drink and ale poured through the floorboards on to Pip and Toad.

"Uurgh!" said Pip.

"Sshhh!" hissed Toad. "Come on. We should get up to

the annex."

But something held them back. As they were about to leave they realized that Jarvis had been joined at his table. Toad pushed his face up to the gap to see who it was.

"Hector Stubbs!" he whispered to Pip, his eyes wide.

Pip said nothing, but made a gesture with open arms. Who was Hector Stubbs?

"He's another one to look out for," continued Toad. "If there's a raid from the authorities in the night, he'll be the one at the front banging the door down. If there's a fight with the forest folk he'll be the first to stick the knife in. He wants every child under his guard with a sword in one hand and a shield in the other, to build his army, to take up war against the woods. He wants to protect the city, but to do it he wants to take you to war. And woe betide anyone caught concealing children from him."

Pip sneaked a look. The man was stocky and short. He had shoulder-length hair, a broad face, and a downturned mouth. The ornate handle of some kind of weapon was at his waist. His cloak trailed on the floor above them.

The boys listened intently.

"Do you have word of anything?" asked Stubbs. His

words came slowly and menacingly.

Jarvis started to answer, but Stubbs interrupted. "Barman, bring me a drink. Ale will do."

Sam nodded his head. He didn't take too kindly to the man's lack of good manners, but he knew he should be careful.

"I'm ... following a few leads," hissed Jarvis, cowering in his seat. "I may have news before too long."

"Really?" said Stubbs. "I heard a rumor. And the rumor was that you were spending too much time in that forest!"

Jarvis shrank into his seat. Esther was concealed inside his cloak and she lay still with her eyes closed. "You never know where those kids might be hiding. I search everywhere, Mister Stubbs. 'Tis my job."

Stubbs carried on, dismissing Jarvis's mumblings. "Some people think that you might be trading children with those forest freaks and that you're making a fool of me in the process. I even heard you'd got yourself a little feathered companion, just like those darned witches." Stubbs paused, studying the intricate carving on his tankard and swilling beer around his mouth. "If I find out you're dealing with those monsters, I'll hang you at the city gates. Do you understand me?"

"You have my word, sir," whispered Jarvis.

"I want those kids, and soon. That's what you're here for."

Pip and Toad turned to look at each other. Their eyes met. Their mouths stayed shut.

They left the cellar and climbed the stairs in candlelit secrecy.

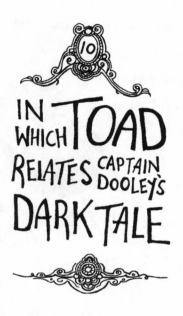

IN WHICH TOAD RELATES CAPTAIN DOOLEY'S DARK TALE

In a short while Pip was in bed. He wondered what was happening in the orphanage and despite all of its troubles he wished he was back there.

Toad kicked off his boots and climbed under his rug.

"You've taken your boots off."

"Oh, I don't bother with the old man's rule. I can have my feet together before he's even woken," Toad grinned.

They talked away into the night, the moon piercing through a slit in the curtain. Toad told dark tales in the silvery light: of the wood creatures and their trickery, of how the witches turned the milk sour in the dairy, sent swarms of flies among the market traders, punished them with boiling rain. Of how the bark demons came in the night, nailing dead rabbits to the doors of those they believed to be harboring children. How they sneaked through the streets in the dead hours, spying at doorways and listening down chimney pots to catch the fireside talk.

"Once," said Toad, sitting up in his bed as he remembered the tale, "a family, the Westleys, were sitting around the fire at night, and an old witch perched on the chimney pot. Her crow had tried every house in the street and this one seemed promising so she had gone to fetch her mistress. They sat

75

together and listened to the children laughing and talking. The parents appeared outside, filling buckets from the water pump, unaware that they were being watched. The old hag took her chance and crawled down the chimney. The Westley children were never seen again."

"How could you know this?"

"A neighbor was watching from across the street, too frightened to move from their own home or raise the alarm."

Pip pulled his blankets up farther. He found Toad's stories terrifying. It wasn't just the tales themselves but Toad's way of telling them, as if he somehow enjoyed it.

"Who is Captain Dooley?" he asked, thinking that some other subject might ease him into sleep.

"Oh, that old story." Toad had hoped he'd forgotten. It wasn't that he didn't want to tell Pip, it was just that he could see that Pip was already frightened.

But perhaps it was better that he knew.

"In the early years a toymaker named Von Shteppel worked in the town. His shop still sits in the square, except that now it's boarded up and has been for many, many years. Without knowing it, he crafted a toy from

Spindlewood. He gave it to his daughter. One day, Annie
Von Shteppel was chased through the woods by witches.
While running to hide from her pursuers she lost her doll,
a solid figure of a soldier from the civil war. Captain
Dooley, she called him. But unbeknownst to Annie, the
Spindlewood curse ran through his woody veins and
he betrayed her. When the witches found him, he told them
where she was hiding. And no matter where she ran, they
found her.

"They kept hold of that little wooden figure until he led them to all the children in the hollow. Some escaped and some didn't, but in the end, like all favorite toys, it seems that Captain Dooley himself became lost again."

A shiver ran down Pip's spine.

"Is that a true story?" he asked. "Does Captain Dooley really exist?"

"Maybe he does and maybe he doesn't!" said Toad. "I couldn't tell you for sure. I can only tell you what was told to me. But one thing I can tell you, Pip. We must find Frankie Duprie before Jarvis does.

"But first things first. Tomorrow, I need to show you our escape route from the tavern. It takes us into the city. Good night," said Toad, and he was asleep before Pip had even closed his eyes.

"Good night," murmured Pip, knowing that his haunting dream would soon return.

IN WHICH A HIDDEN PART OF THE HOLLOW IS NOW REVEALED

The biggest problem was Toad's father, Sam. He wouldn't approve of them leaving the tavern. But that didn't suit Toad, he was far too adventurous. Pip had come to notice that Toad wasn't one for staying still. He was always on the go, always had a plan or a tale to tell. If he was upstairs he would find a reason to go down. Never in the same place for long, despite being cooped up in the house.

Pip was the opposite: much more laid back, but happy to tow along. In a short time Pip felt himself growing close to Toad. He had never had a brother or a sister and he soon began to enjoy the companionship that came with his newfound friend.

"We go at night," said Toad. "I know it's dangerous, but that's when my father is busy. He won't miss us."

"I'm with you," said Pip, biting his lip, and they shook hands as he drummed up the bravery from deep inside himself.

They said good night to Sam as they had become accustomed to doing. They took food and drink to the annex and left fluffed-up cushions in their beds so it looked like they were curled up asleep, in case Sam should check on them in the early hours. Then they put on warm clothes and crept into the cellar when they knew Sam was up to his eyes in customers.

Going down was easy to start with. There was a circular wooden drain cover in the cellar of the inn. Toad stood by the opening with the lid pulled back, inviting Pip to step down onto the ladder.

Pip disappeared into the abyss, bringing life to the

depths with his torch. Toad followed him in, taking a last look around the cellar to make sure he hadn't left any clues. He balanced the drain cover on his head, hatlike, and let it lower into place as he descended. The shaft of torchlight disappeared from the cellar.

The drains were deep and dark and long. The ceiling above was neatly vaulted and below the ladder was a short walkway. Cold drafts sent shivers through their bodies.

Just ahead was a length of rope attached to a loose fitting on the wall.

"Pull on it," said Toad, "and keep on pulling."

Pip tugged away and something heavy resisted at the other end.

"Keep going," said Toad.

Eventually a small wooden boat appeared through the darkness. Two oars lay neatly inside.

Toad smiled. "It's mine," he said. "You didn't think I stayed up there all the time, did you?"

"Does your father know?"

"Of course. It's my best chance of escape should the need arise. But he doesn't know that sometimes I sail around the city when he's not around. In the past, lost children have moved through the city this way."

"What if *they* come down here, you know, the authorities or the forest things?" asked Pip.

"Neither the forest nor the city folk know that children move through these catacombs. If they did, this place would be swarming! Anyhow, the forest folk don't like the water."

"Maybe the Duprie girl is down here!" suggested Pip.

"I've already checked. I've spent hours on end

searching. I'm sure she's not. I don't think it would suit her! Too dark and damp. You can't last long down here without light."

Without saying anything else they both climbed into the boat. Toad took control and steered the boat, showing his skill as an oarsman. The drains mirrored the streets, going this way and that in a brick-filled maze. Pip sat perched at the prow with the lamp held out, illuminating the oncoming darkness.

Toad was reeling out information. "Now we're under the blacksmith's. We've just passed the priory. There's the overflow from the river. We take a right here." Toad plowed down with one oar into the swirling black of the water.

Drips fell from above and the sound of their tiny landings echoed through the tunnels.

Out of the blue a question popped out of Pip's mouth. "Where is your mother, Toad?" He didn't mean to say it out loud, but it had been sitting there in his throat and then it lunged out.

Toad stopped rowing. The boat idled along under its own steam for a short way and Pip turned to look at his friend, casting the light across his face.

"She was taken when I was young. By the forest folk. Father never speaks of it. She died trying to protect me from them. I survived and she didn't. I remember nothing!"

"I'm sorry," said Pip. "I shouldn't have said anything. I just ..."

"It's all right," said Toad. "You were bound to ask at some point. I guess we've both had a hard time in our own way. Keep your eye up ahead, there's a turn soon." And nothing more was said.

Pip began to shiver. It was cold down here and the farther they went, the colder it seemed. He held the base of the lamp in his hands to warm them.

"Freezing, eh?" said Toad.

"Just a bit," said Pip. He wanted it to look like he wasn't bothered but he was shivering uncontrollably.

"Use this," said Toad, throwing him a blanket from the bottom of the boat. Pip wrapped himself up, keeping his torch arm held out.

"We're away from the buildings now," said Toad. "Underneath the square. We have to get out soon. When we reach the ladder give me the nod and I'll pull in."

Pip looked into the dark. The way ahead was barred with a steel grille, allowing the water to carry on but without space for small boats or boys. To the left he saw a laddered shape emerge from the gloom.

"We're here."

They pulled in and tethered the boat to the wooden ladder, leaving the torch and the blanket behind.

Pip stood behind Toad and waited for the nod, his heart thumping inside his chest. To hear of forest creatures was one thing, but to see them for real was another thing entirely.

12

AT WHICH POINT BLACK SHAPES FILL THE SKY AND HIDING BECOMES NECESSARY

Toad's head pushed the drain cover upward and his eyes
peered into the darkness of the
streets, still lined with snow.

CLUNK!

Before he could lift
any farther the drain
cover was bashed

back into place, thumping his head.

"Ouch!"

Toad rubbed his head before taking a look. Jarvis's carriage! Who else would be rumbling through the streets at this hour?

They would have to be extra careful.

When the carriage disappeared through the dark arches they emerged quickly, taking cover in the safety of the long shadow from the tallest buildings.

Something flew above, its shadow sweeping across the square. They stopped and Toad pulled them into another shadow in the recess of a church archway.

"Did you see that?"

"I saw *something*," whispered Pip. "What was it?"

Toad pointed upward. Clinging to the side of a nearby tower was a black shape. What looked like a ragged bat wing was draped across the stone. A closer look revealed two spindly arms hooked into the brickwork.

"Is that what I think it is?" asked Pip.

"Witches," murmured Toad.

Pip felt his stomach roll over. Nerves pulled at his body and a sickness stirred inside him.

"It won't be alone," hissed Toad, his eyes pinned above. They watched and waited.

Soon the sky was peppered with black shapes. They moved quickly, darting and swooping in circles, searching through the air. Pip did not wish to see their faces or their gnarled and twisted hands, but they were close and their features became clear. Whooshing through the archways and gliding over the rooftops, they stopped here and there to cling to the buildings like bats. The boys shrank farther back, deep into the shadows.

"I've never seen so many," whispered Toad. "They must have got word of something. Are you sure you weren't seen when you arrived? They don't come out of the forest in such numbers for no reason."

"I don't know. I don't think so! What do we do now?"

"Sit tight," said Toad. "Something has alerted them. Frankie Duprie may have been seen."

A rolling sound echoed over the stones. It was Jarvis, returning. He circled in the square, almost tipping the carriage over onto two wheels.

Then there was shouting and men appeared on horseback, gazing up at the flock. Tension filled the air.

Something swooped down, drawing close to one of the riders. He swung his torch with his arm held high, hoping to singe the heels of the wood witch.

Then more came, spiraling
down and sending the horses into a
fluster, circling and braying.

Pip and Toad concealed themselves further, dropping
back deeper into the darkness beneath the stone archway
where the snow disappeared, and finding steps leading
into some kind of vault. Complete darkness
surrounded them and they held on to one another.

Compared to this, the boat ride had been a breeze.

Pip got on all fours and felt his way around.

"What are you playing at?" whispered Toad.

"Give me a minute," insisted Pip. "Here," he said at last.

It was another drain cover.

"Good thinking," said Toad, patting him on the back.

They disappeared downward.

"From here we should be able to reach the courtyard

drains," Toad continued. "But the walkway only goes so far." The sound of his voice changed as they entered the catacombs. "We might have to get into the water!"

"I can swim," said Pip. "How about you?"

"Pip, it's freezing in there. You've no idea how cold it will be. But I guess we've no choice."

And so they braved the frozen, stinking, slimy mess of the sewer, shivering manically as they went, with their heads bobbing in the water. They gasped as the cold numbed their bodies. Everything felt heavy, arms and legs like lead weights.

Getting out felt worse than getting in. Their clothes were heavy with the weight of the water and dragged as they pulled themselves up onto the ladder by the boat.

The lamp had gone out. It was blacker than black and they had to hold the oar against the side of the tunneled walls to feel their way. Every drip, every echo, every splash seemed louder than it did in the light. Were they going the right way? They could only hope. But Toad's navigation of the tunnels could be trusted and though it took a good long while before they reached the opening to the cellar at the Deadman's Hand, they eventually made it.

They were soaking, stinking, and frozen.

"So now you know what it feels like to escape from the witches," said Toad, breathing heavily and rubbing himself to keep warm.

"I need my bed," groaned Pip and they disappeared upward into the cellar, where Toad found rags to dry themselves and clothing from a hidden box.

Before long they were warm again and comfortable in their beds. And as silence fell, Pip thought back to his room in the orphanage. The warm bedtime drinks made by Mrs. Tulip, the dreadful bedtime tales read drunkenly by Mister Oakes. Somehow it seemed so much more appealing than it ever had before. He drifted off to sleep, dreaming fitfully of how on earth they were going to find the Duprie girl in the maze of Hangman's Hollow.

For the moment the skies had settled. But the very cautious would have seen that the witches still clung to the buildings like huge insects.

AT WHICH POINT THE IMPORTANCE OF THE DOVES BECOMES APPARENT

Toad climbed the ladder to look through the telescope. Morning had already settled in, the crows were shouting through the woods and the sun had decided to show up. Melting snow dripped from the roof.

Something obscured his vision through the scope. Feathers. *White* feathers. Toad pulled back the cover from around the window and there was a dove, sitting on the edge of the frame. The doves were of no danger to the children, they did not deal with witches or speak with crows. Toad knew this because he had once overheard Esther explaining it to Jarvis. He watched for a while until a second dove appeared, and then another.

"Pip. Are you awake? Pip!"

"I am now," Pip said, sitting up and rubbing his eyes.

"Come look," Toad called. "They're here again. They keep coming. Every day there are more and more."

Pip took a while to come round. They had not returned until late and he was more interested in sleeping right now. Toad was doing it again: unable to keep still, that was Toad.

Ruffled white feathers blocked the window and a gentle cooing sounded. Beaks tapped at the glass and black eyes stared back at them.

Sam bobbed his head round the door. Breakfast was ready.

The day was filled with tiresome work around the tavern. Moving the barrels up and down the cellar steps, some filled to the brim, some empty. Washing the tankards, cleaning the crockery, sweeping and mopping the wooden floor, and replacing the dead candles.

When customers came the boys drifted discreetly into the back. The odd friend of Sam's knew about Toad, but nothing was ever spoken of for safety's sake. Just the occasional "How's things?" or "Everything all right?" inquiry.

By nightfall Pip was exhausted. Such a long day of hard work, and not a breath of the outside world had he seen. He fell head-first into bed, drifting immediately into sleep.

But in his slumber his mind was working. He woke and sat up, shaking Toad in his bed. Toad snored and groaned but Pip persisted. "Toad, wake up!"

"What is it?" mumbled Toad, opening one eye as Pip lit the candle.

"It's the doves!"

"Eh? What? Where?"

"The doves. Where do they roost?"

"Er … the clock tower, I think. Why?"

"I think they're telling you something."

"What?" Toad sat bolt upright with his eyes wide. "Telling us what?"

"The clock tower. It's where Frankie Duprie is!"

"How on earth did you work that one out?" asked Toad, but the more he thought about it, the more it made sense. The doves had started to appear just after the Duprie house had been raided. "It's not going to be easy to get there. But it's worth a try," Toad decided.

And so the following day, they sat planning their way through the city.

Taking the boat through the tunnels to avoid being seen leaving the tavern, they would emerge into the streets and put their plan into action.

They were now only two days from the Winter Carnival: costumes and market stalls and processions, people dancing and parading through the streets as the weird and the wonderful. They would move in disguise.

EXPLAINING HOW PROGRESS WAS MADE DURING THE WINTER CARNIVAL

There was no sight quite so wonderful as the Winter Carnival in the hollow. It was a time when the elders of the city forgot the sadness of their lost children and cheered themselves through the cold months. Smells and sounds brought the darkened streets alive. Roasted meats sizzled in the market square. Breads and fruits of every kind were crammed onto the backs of wheeled carts and parked as

stalls with canopies overhead. Jugglers and fire breathers filled the spaces in between. Choirs sang heartily, huddled into the warmth of their braziers.

The city folk believed that the carnival, with its dances and chants and wild costumes, was a way to ward off the evil of the forest. They mocked the creatures with their beast costumes and played out small acts in the street in which they overcame them with swords and spells.

But it was always such a risk. It tempted the forest creatures out from their holes and it was inevitable that trouble would boil. Often the beasts would mix in with the crowds, wearing cloaks and shrouds, as if in costume. And then they might tear into the people, attacking wildly. Or they would prey on vulnerable revelers as they walked home in small numbers or break into houses, knowing they were empty.

So the guardsmen secured the streets and alleyways on horseback, safeguarding throughout the night and patrolling the inner quarters of the city where the carnival was held. A ring of footmen and mounted guards circled the area. Fires were lit where the forest met the city to ward away evil.

It was early in the evening and the streets were still quiet.

In the shadows something lurked, waiting to emerge. It kept still, concealing its presence.

Hot breath spilled small clouds of nervous fog from its mouth. The hairs on its back were frozen to the touch and the brush of its tail trailed in the snow beneath. Its monstrous head moved shiftily from side to side, baring huge white teeth, and from within it made a sound.

"Are you all right, Pip?"

"Yes, I'm all right, but I'd rather have been at the front."

"You're too small to go at the front. The head needs to be higher than the back end."

"Shush," hissed Pip. "Someone's coming."

A handful of revelers rounded the corner, but were too rowdy to notice the beast lurking in the shadows. They ambled past, laughing and cheering and making merriment.

Pip and Toad would wait for the big parade, and when it came they would merge in and join the festivities, walking alongside the costumed city folk unnoticed.

They would stick with them until they reached the Firefly Bridge, and then break off when they hit the clock tower. They clung on to the hope that Frankie Duprie would be there waiting for them.

From atop a tall roof, Esther was on the lookout, determined to win favor with her master. She had seen something that did not look right. It was the legs. They were too short under that wolf costume. They could only be children!

She drew closer, landing on a nearby post. She would wait until she knew where they were heading, and then she would seek out Jarvis.

Noise came through the darkened streets: clashing of cymbals and banging of drums, voices singing, shouting, laughing. A peer around the corner revealed a gathering crowd, people emerging from their doorways and joining the revelry, torches leading the way. Louder and louder, closer and closer until the narrow streets were crammed with people in every possible disguise to ward off the spoils of winter.

The long snaking shape of a dragon, with what must have been a hundred feet, was walking the street like a huge caterpillar. Toad and Pip sneaked alongside unnoticed, lost in the thrashing of drums and instruments.

They passed through the main square and into the theater courtyard, meeting the procession from the Stage Fright Theatre Company. Pip sneaked a look. He recognized the voices, the storytellers, and a tall woman he had seen, all of them dressed in their costumes.

They continued through the maze of streets and alleys, sometimes struggling to pass through the walkways. As they turned corners others joined them until soon the whole city was walking with them. The noise was deafening.

The boys were jostling for position, struggling along without being able to see, and sweating under the skin of the beast, despite the freezing cold around them. By the time they reached the clock tower they were ready for a rest. Up ahead a square border of stone framed a squat archway, announcing their arrival at their destination.

"Move over to the edge," shouted Pip. "Then we can disappear."

"Harder than you think!" yelled Toad. He was growing tired of steering through the crowd. At times they were almost lifted off their feet by the surge of bodies.

But good fortune came their way when it mattered. A fight broke out, a small scuffle that turned into a brawl, and all eyes were diverted. Some man in a dragonskin had disagreed with a skeleton and they laid into each other awkwardly. Laughter broke as they tipped into a nearby water trough.

All the pushing and shoving had allowed the hog-toothed beast to ease over to the opposite side of the costumed mob. They merged into the shadows of the arches that told them they were right beneath the clock tower.

It was going well. Too well, in fact.

Three figures in gray hooded cloaks and plague masks were following them. Something glinted beneath one of the cloaks. While all about them roared with song and laughter, they simply moved along with the crowd. Not dancing or singing, just waiting for the right moment.

The boys' feet echoed as they moved toward the steps that led up to the clock, shedding the skin of the hog-toothed beast and dragging it along behind. It was a steep climb, hundreds of wide shallow steps that left their knees aching and sore before they were even halfway. They stopped and looked out through a small window. The procession was still passing below them. It looked magical to Pip. Glowing torchlights, costumes, and color and the snow all around them.

But there was no time for admiring the view. "Come on," said Toad, puffing and panting. And they hurried on up. They reached a heavy, low wooden door. It was locked.

"Here," said Pip. "Let me have a go." He drew a small spike of metal from his pocket and scratched at the barrel until it came free.

"Where did you learn to do that?" asked Toad.

Pip stared back with raised eyebrows and said nothing. Instead he turned the handle and a sure smile crossed his face as he felt the lock release and the door slowly open.

A SHORT BIT AT THE END OF CHAPTER FOURTEEN

So eager was he for the hooded followers to catch up that Captain Dooley sat bolt upright in his old cloth sack. "Quickly!" he shouted, his voice rusty and still only half awake. "Not a moment to lose!"

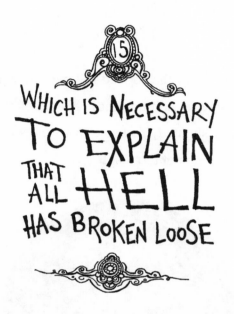

WHICH IS NECESSARY TO EXPLAIN THAT ALL HELL HAS BROKEN LOOSE

A bright moon shone through the large clock face, aiming a pool of light into the lofty space. The timber floor was dry and dusty. Huge cogs and machine parts filled the void they stood in and the children had to crouch and climb to pass through.

A dove fluttered up from the floor, surprising them and making them jump back.

Toad called out gently. "Frankie Duprie, are you there? It's Toad. Sam's boy from the tavern."

There was only silence, but Pip's keen eye spotted her in the corner, behind the turning shapes of cogs and hammers, her eyes shining. As they drew closer to her she spoke not a word. "Come out, Frankie. You're safe now," said Pip, holding out his arms.

With startled eyes she was curled up tight like a spring and wouldn't move.

"It's all right," said Toad. "We'll look after you now. Are there any others?"

She remained silent and shook her head.

Just then the three gray figures burst in. Such a dreadful sight that the young girl screamed out loud.

"Well, well, well. What have we here?" said the first in a rasping male voice.

"How nice," cackled the second. "There's one each."

The first figure pulled back his hood with a hooked hand and showed his scarred face.

"Jarvis!" said Toad under his breath.

"You take the girl, Hogwick," instructed the hook-handed thug. "I'll take the fat one."

111

The second unveiled herself. A sharp-faced old crone, a wood witch if ever there was one. She grabbed Frankie, who was too terrified to move.

Jarvis moved quickly, yanking Toad by the scruff of his neck and pulling him close to his steel hook so that Toad couldn't move without being sliced.

The third didn't speak. He simply removed his cloak so that he could retrieve Pip, but as he did so the children saw that he had a second pair of arms that joined beneath the first. He used a cane but as he prepared to go to work, he seemed agile.

He snaked eerily on his belly into the workings of the clock and inched toward Pip, clutching and grasping at his feet. His face edged closer: one eye pale and silvery, the other deep and dark. Pip sat tight, hoping that the creature wasn't small enough to climb all the way into his hiding place. But the thing managed to circle his cane around Pip's ankle and began to drag him out by his boot.

"Come to Papa Roach, dear boy, don't be frightened."

Pip scraped along the dusty floor, yelping and kicking. Pulling on the cane with two hands, the spidery man swung out a grasping hand. Pip ducked and the thing yelped in pain as his hand struck a vertical timber, the fingers making a cracking sound. With only a second or two of freedom, Pip took a chance and headed up into the workings of the clock, disappearing fast.

"Leave it. Bolt the door and we'll come back for him," yelled Jarvis, and Roach worked some trickery with the lock before the three of them thundered down the steps with Frankie and Toad held fast.

"Call the others. We need help. Don't let the little one get away," Roach insisted.

Pip listened carefully, trying to calm his breathing, and found a spot where he could spy the street. The man with the cane was in trouble. His hand looked broken.

As they disappeared out of sight Pip sat helplessly, knowing that the hooded gray figures would disappear into the now-empty streets with his comrades concealed beneath their filthy cloaks.

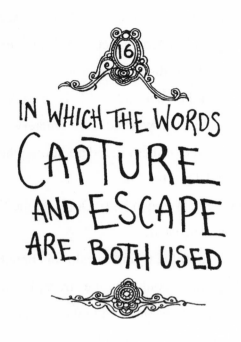

IN WHICH THE WORDS CAPTURE AND ESCAPE ARE BOTH USED

Toad and Frankie felt themselves being shuffled along,
Frankie beneath the witch's cloak and Toad beneath
Jarvis's, with the hook held so near to his face that he only
dared move his legs. They could hear a horse and two sets
of footsteps approaching, but when Jarvis pulled the hood
from his head they stood back and let him pass. They
neglected to notice that beneath their disguises his
companions were forest dwellers.

116

Round corners, down darkened alleys, up a small rise of steps and onto the flat again. Then out from beneath the cloaks and bundled upward, shoved and dragged awkwardly until their feet found a platform and they passed through a small opening into a damp-smelling space with a rotted seat. The clang of a door. The turn of a key.

Their eyes adjusted. It was immediately obvious to Toad that they were in Jarvis's black carriage. Above the locked handles on the doors were windows barred with cold hard iron.

Frankie began to weep, but Toad was too furious to be frightened. He leaped to his feet and pulled hard at the bars.

"Let me out, you freaks."

The carriage rolled along, slipping through the dark streets, and Toad pulled so hard on the iron bars that the whole thing shook from side to side. Jarvis's grin grew wide. He had what he wanted, and he knew there was at least another child on the move, something to make his searches more exciting. He had been right all along. They were there: You just had to know where to look.

"It's all just a matter of time," he said to Roach. "I always capture them in the end. Nice work, Esther," he added, and she sat proudly at the front of the carriage, preening herself.

But Roach wasn't happy. He nursed what he was sure were broken fingers, tucking them under his arm and wincing in pain.

"Not to worry," grinned Jarvis. "You still have three hands left. I only got the one!"

And they rolled along, the pumpkin rocking from side to side and Toad's cries going unheard by the city folk.

The procession moved on, back to the market square where the stalls poured out their drinks and handed out their food. Jarvis stuck to the outside edge of the city. He was a traitor and the biggest of cowards.

Toad watched helplessly as they passed through the rusted broken gate into the forest. The streets and houses became pathways and trees. The silence of the streets became the echoing call of crows and the haunting howl of wolves through the spiny winter trees.

And now the witches came flocking to look at the caged animals. They swarmed around the carriage, pulling on the bars, and peering in.

"Ooh look, there's a pretty one and an ugly one," they cackled.

"Let us go," growled Toad. Frankie had stayed quiet all along, petrified into silence. She pulled her shawl tightly around herself and leaned away from the barred window.

Gnarled fingers clung to the bars and hands reached in.

"Such beautiful hair and soft skin. These will make good prisoners."

But Toad just yelled louder. "Let us out, Jarvis," he yelled, and pushed harder against the sides of the carriage until it almost tipped over.

Frankie lifted her head and she was about to blurt something out, but a jolt of the carriage stopped her and the words trailed off into a scream. The coach crashed down on one side and Toad saw the rear left-hand wheel go rolling past.

"Ahh, curses," grunted Jarvis, and his grin turned quickly upside down as he fell from his seat and he and Roach ended up on the ground tied in a knot, not knowing whose limbs were whose.

Toad's weight had sent him hurtling through the rotten base of the carriage and he landed on the forest floor with his head still inside the cab. His eyes lit up at the opportunity.

There was much commotion as the witches found their feet in the darkness, pulling each other from the thorns and thickets.

"Quick," Toad whispered to Frankie. "It's our only chance. Follow me." And they squeezed their way out from under the carriage into the dark depths of the woods.

It had not entered the mind of the forest dwellers that the children could have escaped. Quite some time passed while they pulled at the broken wheel and struggled to lift it onto the axle, all with no success. It was only a sudden realization that Toad had stopped hurling insults that made Jarvis look inside … to see that his catch was missing.

"Aaaargh … they've escaped. Those disgusting little city rats have escaped!"

As Jarvis's scream echoed eerily into the trees, the carriage was soon forgotten and the searchers dispersed. But by now Toad and Frankie were already far from the scene of the accident, spilling into the thick of the forest.

RELATING THE CIRCUMSTANCES OF PIP'S NEXT MOVE

Pip had no idea what Roach had done with the lock, but after minutes of trying he was sure that he couldn't release it. Brute strength was out of the question. The solid wooden door was too much for Pip's tiny frame. And if he hung around much longer they would return and snap him up.

Pip's mind began to turn. When they had arrived, Frankie was in there but the door was locked. How had she gotten in there? There must be a way. He flustered around nervously, feeling the walls in the half light. And there it was, in the far corner, caked in dust: a small hatch in the floor with a lip to grab hold of and pull.

As Pip lowered himself down he found himself back on the staircase that led up to the locked clock tower doorway. Within moments he was creeping through the hollow. There was a hum of noise from the celebrations in the distance and every now and then someone would come skipping by or a group would wander past in a drunken fashion. But for the most part it was deathly quiet.

Up above, shapes were circling. Word must already have filtered into the forest of Pip's narrow escape, and the scouts were out. Without Toad he wasn't entirely sure which drain holes were useful to him or indeed where they would take him. But on foot he could find his way.

He slipped up an alley that he was sure would take him back to the theater courtyard. From there he already knew the route to the tavern, and if he could get there, he could find the forest gate.

In his head he was already there, but he had not planned to stumble into someone. His eagerness had tripped him up.

At first the man apologized and tried to move past, but on realizing it was a child he grew shocked and anxious and immediately eager to help him.

"What are you doing? It's not safe to move at night, you should know that. Where are you from?" As they passed into the light at the corner of the theater courtyard the face of a kind old man became clear.

He took Pip's hand. "Quick," he pleaded. "To safety!"

Pip knew the scouts would be circling above and felt he had no choice but to follow, stumbling awkwardly in the dark.

The man pulled Pip through a door and into a small low cottage with a rounded window, where he yanked on the shutters so that Pip could not be seen from outside. Inside there was a small table and a rickety chair, a fire burned gently in the hearth, and a pot bubbled over the flames. The smell was delicious.

"There, you see. Safety at last!" the man announced. "Oh, do forgive me, I have not introduced myself. My name is Crumb ... Jed Crumb. Or Old Jed, as they often call me. And you are?"

"Pip, sir. My name is Eddie Pipkin, but my friends call me Pip."

"In that case, young man, I shall consider myself a friend of yours and address you accordingly. You must be starving, Pip. All that escaping is hungry work, yes?" He returned with a plate of cakes and buns so big it dwarfed the table. And then hot drinks and more food seemed to appear from nowhere, accompanied by delicious smells that made Pip think of Sam's food at the tavern.

"Eat up," the man said. "There's plenty more where that came from."

"Thank you most kindly, sir. But I don't have much

time for food," said Pip. "My friends have been taken by Mister Jarvis and his kin. I must reach them."

"You mean the forest people?"

"Yes, sir."

"How many are there of you? Where did you spring from?"

Suddenly Pip became aware that the man might not be on his side. Of course, he seemed friendly enough, but what if … No, surely not. He had helped him get to safety. But he was asking Pip for information he did not want to give. What if it meant that Sam got into trouble?

"I've been hiding in the clock tower," said Pip. "The doves bring me bread and I collect water from the spouts in the dead of night."

"Poor thing," the man said with his head to one side. "You must stay here, and for as long as you like. I shall make up a bed for you."

"No, really," Pip insisted. "I cannot rest until I find my friends. Something could be happening to them right now."

"But these streets are not safe, especially at this hour." The man tried to place a reassuring hand on Pip's shoulder as he moved to the door.

"I'm sorry," Pip said, "but I have to find them."

"No!" he roared as Pip reached for the handle. The man's voice burned like fire. His eyes turned from green to red, then bright orange, and his white hair singed with the same fiery hot colors. His mouth opened wide and now Pip could see that his teeth were sharp and pointed. All the kindness drained from him, his features changing in a moment, his hands growing into long-fingered claws.

Pip fumbled at the door and slipped through it, realizing in that instant that the man was a creature from the forest, sent into the city to trap him. For a moment he had no idea where to turn, holding on to the door to prevent him from following outside. Then he lunged across the street into the dark alley they had come from and lost himself in darkness.

He bolted, foxlike, into the dark. His mind raced. Whose home had the forest dweller used to lure him in? Surely not his own. Perhaps he had raided the house of some poor woman and had her tied up in the kitchen. Maybe he lived in secrecy as a city dweller and a spy. Maybe other forest types could change themselves into human form and lived in the same way. How could he ever trust anyone again? All these thoughts and more invaded his head as he raced onward.

Pip's mind tracked back. The last time he had run so fast was making his escape from Mister Oakes at the harbor. If only he had known what he knew now, he would have turned back for sure.

Old Jed followed awkwardly, bent double, his back arching upward. His wolfish moon eyes stared into the black, searching desperately. He couldn't let go of his prize, not when he'd had him right there in his grasp.

He pulled himself into a shadow and drew his cloak around him to conceal his presence. If he waited long enough, perhaps Pip would emerge from somewhere.

But it was Old Jed who was spotted first. Torchlight rang down the alleyway, voices broke the air in two, and guardsmen in uniform appeared. The forest dweller was caught, rabbitlike, in the orange light. For a moment he was still, then he tried to dart away, but an attack ensued and a shrill cry pierced the night.

Pip was a breath away, motionless in a bricked-up doorway, watching as wood witches came flocking from above to come to the caller's aid. Something lunged past him toward the chaos, something that stank heavily of damp and trees and moss. It was gone in a moment, and he watched it pass into the light of the torches: some kind of clawed beast that speared its long fingers at the guards from beneath a red cloak.

Pip soon realized it was a battle between forest and city. Clangs of shields and spears, claws raking walls and metal, horses trampling. He was entranced by the scene, almost unable to move, but he knew he should use the confusion to flee from sight.

He stepped out and risked being

caught by the light. The bedlam was enough to distract the fighters as he moved away, still unable to understand that what he saw was real.

He moved backward, his hands raking their way across the walls, and it soon became apparent that he had steered himself toward the woods. He looked down to see a pair of rusted broken gates. Knotted and gnarled tree bark reached down toward him. The streets had gone and the buildings had been replaced with twisting trunks and branches. At his feet the cold bit into his toes through a bed of leaves and snow. There was no mistaking it. Pip was in the forest.

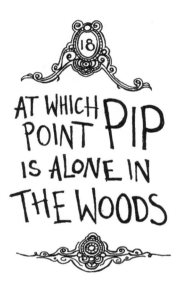

AT WHICH POINT PIP IS ALONE IN THE WOODS

Perhaps it was Pip's wild imagination, but as soon as he felt the forest floor beneath his feet he sensed that the trees were against him. That their roots twisted and turned and tried to trip his feet. That the branches above seemed to reach out to grab him or scratch at his face and tear at his clothes.

And somehow he had begun to feel sleepy. There was

some drowsy, dreamy feel about the forest, almost as if sorcery was in the air, filtering between the trees like fog and bringing a strange earthy scent that was somehow pleasant and hypnotic.

Pip pushed on. He dared not call out and the night grew darker as he went farther in and the light from the city faded. Where should he look? Which way should he turn? There was more chance that he would be caught than that he would find Frankie and Toad. He stumbled and fell and the strange scent grew stronger, making him sleepier.

Up ahead, there was a clearing lit by a shaft of moonlight. Pip stopped and rested a moment, listening to the noises in the woods. Distant cawing and cackling, the creak and twist of trees. Who knows what could be happening to Toad and Frankie? He looked down to see the prettiest-looking flower. The smell was so strong now that he felt himself dozing as he sat. His head tilted down, making his body jerk, and his own movement woke him.

In that instant he realized what was happening. It was the scent of the winter flowers making him tired. Of course! This must be how so many of the children had

been caught in the very beginning and no one had ever realized.

Pip ripped the sleeve from his shirt so that he had something to cover his nose and mouth before he soldiered on. The smell tried to drag him down, but he was determined to fight. He picked up freezing handfuls of snow and rubbed the snow into his face to keep himself awake.

But the farther he went the more chance there was of being seen. The nose of the wolf would sniff him out, or the eye of the crow would find him. The craftiness of the witch would catch him. Still he carried on, plowing through the snow.

After some time he spied a shape up ahead, a rounded silhouette. It was the pumpkin carriage, abandoned in the middle of nowhere. The horse was still tethered and shuffled on its hooves, whinnying and braying and breathing its clouds of fog into the still air.

What had happened here? Pip's heart began to beat fast. Had his friends already been beaten by some disaster?

Pip realized that he was missing Toad's company. He thought of the way that Toad made him laugh, of his clumsy blustering ways and of all the other things that made Toad who he was. How he kept Pip awake at night with dark tales of the hollow, or woke him up early when he was worn out. Pip feared that he might have lost the only person in his life that he had ever really felt close to.

At the same time that Pip found the carriage, Jarvis and Roach had a stroke of luck.

"What is that?" said Roach. He had sent Fenris searching up ahead and there was a flurry of activity. More wolves joined him as his snout poked into the hollow of a tree and howls filled the air.

Roach and Jarvis hurried forward. Jarvis held up the

torch with his one good hand and lit the scene.

"Get back," said Roach, protecting his battered hand by nursing it in a spare armpit. "Let me in."

And there inside the trunk were the sleeping figures of Toad and Frankie, worn down by the scent of the forest flowers.

"Got 'em!" Roach grinned. Fenris grabbed each by their collar and pulled their sleeping bodies out onto the snowy floor of the forest. The other wolves leered over them and licked their lips.

"Away," growled Roach. "These are not for your picking."

"Hurry! We must make haste," said Jarvis. "These young ones will make fine prisoners. The keep has been empty far too long."

Howls filled the air and the call of the crows joined them from the city streets. The witches knew what that meant, they knew the children had been found and captured.

In a swarming spiraling flock they spun upward and swarmed back toward the treetops.

*

Pip stopped and listened to the deafening howling and

cawing. As he gazed up into the moonlit space above he saw the black flock returning, and a chill ran through his already freezing bones.

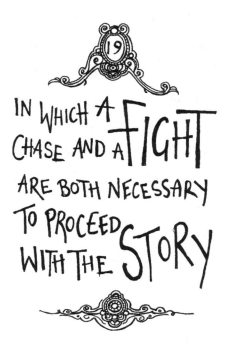

19

IN WHICH A CHASE AND A FIGHT ARE BOTH NECESSARY TO PROCEED WITH THE STORY

It was a rapid assembly of the Stone Circle. The wolves plowed through the snow, moving swiftly between the trees in packs of five and six.

A sweeping, whooshing sound whistled through the air as the witches flocked downward like rapidly falling autumn leaves. The crows drew up behind them, spreading their cloaks as they landed on the shoulders of their companions. Other creatures climbed out from their holes and scratched their way across the branches.

By now Pip had untethered the horse and managed to climb on to its back by using a step from the broken carriage. At first the horse resisted, braying and rearing up on its hind legs, but Pip held on. If there was one thing he felt comfortable doing it was handling a horse. "Whooaa, girl," he said, steadying her nerves. He put his arms around her neck and whispered something that seemed to calm her down. Then he began to steer her through the trees.

Though it was the last thing he wanted to do, Pip headed in the direction of the howls. He knew that if he did not get there in time he would not see Toad and Frankie again.

"The boy is coming. He's almost there!" called out Captain Dooley, who was now wide awake. "Hurry, hurry. Faster, faster!" And he grew so excited at the prospect of the new prisoners that he caused the old cloth sack to dislodge itself from its position and it fell, unseen, through a hole in the floor of the old attic.

Pip was thundering through the forest now, getting to know his newfound companion. He held a sturdy stick in his right hand and beat at the twigs and branches, ducking and bobbing his head here and there.

The sleeping children were being carried by the wolves. The whole forest followed, gazing upon the youngsters.

A clap of thunder rumbled up above and lightning struck a nearby tree, sending a flash of light and fire into the Stone Circle.

The thunder and lightning had startled Pip's horse and he struggled to keep control, holding on tight to her neck and feeling her hot breath cloud his face.

He stumbled into the clearing and suddenly he was faced with the Stone Circle and the crowd that huddled tightly around it, but the horse was going so fast that she plowed into the tangle of wolves and witches, and the crows lifted into the air in fear, scattering amongst the trees.

The horse trampled the fire in the confusion and Pip

saw that Frankie and Toad were standing motionless, propped up against a pillar. The horse's rear end circled as Pip held on to her neck: She kicked out, and Roach and Jarvis were thrust into a nearby thicket. The wolves snapped at her ankles, but they were no match for the stature and strength of the black steed.

Pip pulled desperately at Toad and stirred his drowsy state. "Quick!" he roared. "Climb up!" He was not going to let go of his friend, not now that he had found him. Toad was startled into action: Half-roused and half-asleep, he began to pull Frankie along with him. They kicked out at the wolves and the witches and used the crumbling stone of the surrounding ruin to climb up onto the horse.

The crows were descending again, pecking from above. Hogwick darted forward, keeping out of range of the horse's hooves. Pip grabbed a flaming branch from the fire and swiped at the beastly limbs and crows' beaks.

The horse continued to circle, her three passengers clinging to each other for dear life. With a jolt, she shot forward and a chase ensued through the trees. The crack and splinter of wood echoed beneath them as they bolted toward the light from the city.

"Don't look back!" cried Pip. But they did. The wolves were struggling to keep up with the horse. The witches darted skillfully between the spaces in the trees. Toad grabbed Pip's flaming branch and began to beat at them as they came. Frankie was sandwiched between them, with her arms round Pip's waist. She tucked her head between his shoulder blades, kicking her legs out at whatever was there.

They slid across the horse's back, their feet digging in to hold on. A clawed hand dug its grip into Toad's shoulder. He looked back to see Pugg straining to hold on to him, preventing him from turning round to attack her with the stick. But the low bough of a nearby tree cut her short, knocking her out completely.

Hogwick was trailing way behind. All she could do was hurl a spell in their direction, but it was drowned out by the shouts and dissipated into thin air.

Jarvis was furious. "That's my horse, you thieves!"

Roach was determined not to give in. He crawled on five limbs, drumming over the forest floor and drawing close as the witches continued to slow the horse down until she was almost standing still.

Pip dug his feet into her side. "Come on, girl. Just a little more." They were almost out of the woods.

Screaming and cawing and cackling and howling surrounded them. The children were pulled and scratched and tugged, but somehow they held on.

Toad was swiping the stick with all his might. "No one is going to make a forest boy out of me!" he yelled.

Abruptly the sound of hooves on cobbles could be heard and they spilled out through the broken rusted gates into the city streets. But that did not stop the chase. Still the witches held on.

Roach was gaining on them fast. He was so determined that he had now forgotten his injuries

and he tore across the cobbles like lightning.

Pip didn't know the city well enough and the maze of streets was a blur, but Frankie knew this part better than anyone. They were near to the Duprie house. She piped up and began to shout out directions from her position in the middle. "Left, right, straight on. Heads down!" she warned, as they entered the skinny, tunneled passageway of Puddle Snake Alley. It was so tight that the horse struggled to pass through, and as it did it scraped off any hangers-on. A heap of witches lay scattered at the entrance to the walkway, but some flew overhead and waited at the other end, circling like vultures, ready to swoop on the emerging riders.

Out came the steaming breath of the horse, followed by her head and then her bare back. The children had gone, lost in the black of the tunnel. The horse bolted through the streets alone, sweating and braying and slipping on the icy surface of the cobbles.

A swarm of witch life filtered into the narrow space from both ends, searching the darkness.

"They're in here!" screamed Jarvis, but no one could see anything.

Roach scrabbled upside down along the walls, feeling his way along every brick.

"Nothing!" he roared. "Nothing at all!"

Witches hung like bats from the ceiling, searching every inch of the void where the children had disappeared. And when that proved fruitless out they went, filing through the streets like ants until finally the streets grew quiet and soon the only sound that could be heard was the doves in the nearby clock tower.

"Where are they?" screeched Jarvis as he stood in the silence of the market square with his arms held up in despair. "Where have they gone?"

AT WHICH POINT WE UNCOVER THE WHEREABOUTS OF THE ESCAPEES

Silence returned to the streets. There was no cawing or cackling or squawking or the thunderous pounding of feet. Just stillness.

Toad lifted the drain cover in Puddle Snake Alley and the whites of his eyes broke the darkness.

"Have they gone?" whispered Pip.

"There's no sign of anything," said Toad.

148

"It's freezing down here," said Frankie. "I want to go home."

"You can't go home," said Toad. "The old place is empty. You'll have to return with us, to the tavern. We should head there now. All that matters is that you're safe. We'll have you fed and watered in no time."

They climbed down the wooden ladder and disappeared into the depths of the tunnels, while above their heads the wood folk filtered back into the forest without the slightest clue of where the children had gone.

There was no boat, but their branch was still burning at least, and there was a good length of walkway before the friends would have to get into the water to cover the last stretch.

The light petered out as they felt their way through the darkness. They stopped to catch their breath, puffing clouds of white air. Pip blew on the branch to stop the flame from dying, and when the brick path ran out they braved the freezing water for the last stretch of the journey.

They emerged soaking and frozen into the darkness of the tavern cellar. Sam was right there, and when he heard the drain cover rattling at his feet he panicked and grabbed a pitchfork. He stood there waiting, shaking. What would appear? Something from the forest? But no, it was the face of his only son.

Sam had been so frantic with worry and despair, and unable to talk to anyone about it, that he dropped to his knees when he saw Toad. Relief washed over him and tears sprang uncontrollably from his eyes.

"I've never been so worried," grunted Sam. "Look at the state of you! Where on earth have you been?"

"If it hadn't been for Pip, you would have never seen the three of us again." Toad grinned.

"Three?" quizzed Sam.

"Yes, three. There are three of us now," began Toad, "There is someone we want you to meet. Someone who was worth the risk."

And out climbed Frankie Duprie. Almost as tiny as Pip, with torn and ragged clothes that matched the scars on her face. Shattered and worn, soaked to the skin, and frozen to the bone.

"Frankie!" said Sam.

He was shocked into silence and he stood a moment while he took in the scene around him, realizing what the children must have been through.

Pip had never seen an adult cry before. For a moment he didn't understand it, and then a feeling washed over him, a feeling he had never had before. A warmth that came from the people around him, a hum of companionship, a glow of safety and kinship. Of all the things he could have felt right there and then, and after all he had been through, he did not expect to feel like this at all. He felt himself holding back his own tears.

"We must get news to your parents, Frankie," Sam said. "But you must stay here for your own safety. Toad, make up another bed. Pip, show Frankie the annex. Go quietly. Make a bath. I'll cook."

Sam smiled away to himself as he warmed up the stove and began to conjure food from his kitchen.

Anger stirred in the forest. Harsh exchanges broke the eerie silence of the woods. "Assemble the Stone Circle," growled Jarvis. "Bring yourselves to the reckoning. Some of you will pay for this."

In a short while the tavern was busy again, and in the way that Sam had always loved in the past: with children's voices and the sound of small feet parading up and down the stairs.

For the first time in a long time Pip didn't dream of his

parents, of the faceless figures of his mother and father that jostled him in his sleep. Instead, he dreamed of the hollow. But it wasn't the same hollow. It was a peaceful one, without a forest, or dark corners where strange things lurked or preyed. And in the dream he sat at the fire, cozy and warm, and Sam was there and Frankie and Toad. They talked and laughed and told dark tales into the early hours, and they were scared but it was a good scared, not a bad one. A safe and warm scared.

He had not slept like that in such a long time.

A SHORT NOTE TO AVOID THE COMFORT THAT COMES WITH AN ALMOST HAPPY ENDING

The old place was filthy. Derelict, you might call it. No one had been here for some time. It was not the safest of buildings in the hollow, and repairs would have to be made if it was to be habitable. The plaster was cracked and damp in places, and the river came too high up the brickwork. So far in fact that if you looked out from the window you might think you were looking out from the inside of a boat as the water washed up against the sides.

Stonework and debris had fallen from the attic,
tumbling down the chimney and dropping inside
the hearth.

A hand reached in and searched
through the junk. A wooden box, a
pile of old books and papers, and
the soot-covered remains of an
old cloth sack.

Amongst the odds and ends in
the sack, the hand found a small
wooden figure of a soldier from the
civil war. It dusted him down until his scuffed
black boots shone again and his jacket was red once
more. Apart from the flaking paint and the bent feather in
his hat, he looked as smart as could be.

And for now he sat in silence on the mantelpiece,
with his eyes fixed on the doorway so that he could see
who came and went. He knew full well that when the
moment was right and he had something to say he would
go ahead and let out his secrets. Secrets of the children
from Hangman's Hollow.

Chris Mould

Chris Mould went to art school at the age
of sixteen. During this time, he did various
jobs, from delivering papers to cleaning
and cooking in a kitchen. He loves his work
and likes to write and draw the kind
of books that he would have liked to have
on his shelf as a boy. He is married with two
children and lives in Yorkshire, England.

And now an excerpt from book two
in the Spindlewood Tales trilogy,

PIP AND THE TWILIGHT SEEKERS

WHICH EXPLAINS THAT WHEN THE BLIZZARD STOPPED, THE BEDLAM WOULD BEGIN

The winters are long, here in the hollow. Cold and thick and deep. Snowstorms sweep across the valley and through the city, tearing through the streets between the houses and piling drifts up against the doorways, whistling between the trees and lacing thick frost around the trunks and branches.

The clawed hands and spindly claws of the forest creatures had retreated into the barky holes of the Spindlewood trees. The thick white of the forest floor was free of their cloven hoof marks and lumbering footprints. Even Jarvis, the city warden, sat cooped up in his hovel, unable to venture out in search of strays. He hated children and he would stop at nothing to be rid of them. But right now, his carriage lay broken upon the ground, its axle crushed, the loose wheel discarded and covered in snow.

No one had moved for some time. Not since those three children had escaped the evils of the forest by the skin of their teeth and had Jarvis and the rest of the woodsfolk screaming after them.

But now the wind stopped. The hurling of snow and chilled air came to an abrupt halt. Beneath the deep drifts were shattered roof tiles and broken chimney pots. Fractured branches from nearby trees poked out like spring buds. But this was no growing season. The freezing winter was still waging war against the world.

"Crank up the fire, Esther," urged Jarvis as he sat lazily huddled up to the fireplace with one hand and one hook tucked into his armpits. He watched, amused, as the crow pulled meager twigs from the basket and nosed them into place, dancing around the spits of crackling orange.

Eventually he rose from his chair and hooked back the drab, rotted curtain that framed his frosty window. He breathed on the glass and circled his hand on the pane. "The blizzard has stopped, Esther. It's time to seek out our revenge and lay our hands on those pesky little city rats. We know they're here. I always get my prize in the end," he said proudly, one eye shut and the other squinting out through the glass, his bulbous nose squashing against the pane.

Jarvis had been tracking his mind back through the recent turmoil in the hollow. He'd almost had those three children in his grasp. He'd come so close to putting them in the forest keep. But they'd escaped and now he boiled with anger.

All through the blizzards that had followed after the children's escape, he had sat inside and turned things over in his mind. He could still see them. The smallest was a young boy whom he knew to go by the name of Pip. The next, a young girl, memorable by her rats' tails of hair and ragged clothes. But the biggest, a large boy, was somehow more familiar. That tubby-cheeked face kept coming to him. He'd seen it somewhere before and he knew it would come back to him if he thought long and hard enough.

"Time to venture out, I think," said Jarvis, announcing his next move to Esther.

"But what of the carriage?" begged Esther. "And the broken wheel?"

"I'm going to walk to the tavern, Esther. Something is preying on my mind." Jarvis seemed to be lost in thought.

He was about to step out through the door

when he turned back. He wandered over to the hearth and, lifting his left arm, he sharpened the tip of his hook against the stone lintel. He took a long proud look at its pointed end, gave it a shine with the corner of his black cloak, and then wrapped the cloak around himself and disappeared into the night, leaving deep footprints in the thick of the snow.